This **TWO HOOTS** book belongs to

_____

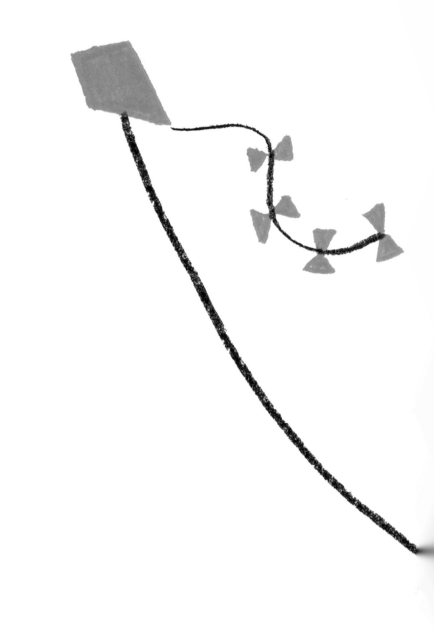

JUSTIN ROBERTS   CHRISTIAN ROBINSON

THE
SMALLEST
GIRL IN
THE CLASS

TWO HOOTS

Hardly anyone noticed young Sally McBrass.

She was the smallest girl in the smallest class.

Yes, her name could be heard in the daily roll call,
and she marched with her books down the same school hall.
But hardly anyone noticed young Sally McBrass.

And they *certainly* didn't know, or at least didn't mention, that Sally was paying extra special attention.

To the abandoned kite with the tangled string.
To the twenty-seven keys on the caretaker's ring.

To the leaves turning gold as they started to fall.
To the time Tommy Torino was tripped in the hall.

She watched as the wildflowers tipped to the light,
and heard the howl of a hound dog late in the night.

She was there when the stray cats who fought in the dark
were surprisingly peaceful in the city car park.

She saw Kevin McKuen get pushed off a slide—
and the first few tears that he wanted to hide.

And she'll never forget that Parents' Day
when Billy's dad suddenly dragged him away.

But through all the mean words and all the cold stares,
nobody noticed that Sally was there.
And they didn't know, or at least didn't mention,
that Sally was paying extra special attention.

She'd seen how a whisper could make someone cower
like a bulldozer crushing through fields of wildflowers.
And it kept piling up, this discarded debris,
those beautiful kites tangled in trees.

So on May the third at twelve twenty-nine,
Sally stepped out of the lunch hall line.

She said, "I'm tired of seeing
this terrible stuff.
Stop hurting each other!
This is enough!"

Now, a few laughed out loud or didn't care
that there was some girl with her hand in the air.

But then something super special happened that day
as Howard O'Henry set down his tray.

Like waves rolling in, one after another—
first Molly rose up, then Michael's twin brother.
It was Tyrone and Terence, then Amanda and Paul,
who pushed out their chairs and stretched their arms tall.

From the friendly lunch lady with the dishes she carted,
to that new Year Three teacher who had only just started.
Yes, everyone there, even Headteacher Claire,
had joined little Sally, fingers high in the air.

And though hound dogs were destined
to howl in the night,
and most stray cat meetings would end up as fights,
and kites would continue to get stuck in trees,
they all felt, for a moment, like the caretaker's keys.

Fastened together with a heavy steel ring
that held all the secrets to unlock everything.

As the world returned to the way that it was,
Sally noticed the difference, as she usually does,
when Billy paused briefly to open the door
for Mrs O'Connell and seventeen more.

Or when Molly scooched over to make some more space
on the choral benches for Ellen and Grace.
These moments that often get taken for granted—
a wildflower appearing that no one had planted.

The swings soon resumed their rhythm and sway,
and day turned to night and night turned to day.

People remembered and would quite often mention
that Sally had been paying extra special attention.
And how the world could transform and a change come to pass
thanks to the smallest girl in the smallest class.

To all those paying
super extra special attention.
—J.R.

To Yvonne.
Thank you for standing up for me.
—C.R.

Published by arrangement with G.P. Putnam's Sons,
an imprint of Penguin Young Readers Group,
a division of Penguin Random House LLC

First published in the US 2014 by G. P. Putnam's Sons
This edition published in the UK 2022 by Two Hoots
an imprint of Pan Macmillan
The Smithson, 6 Briset Street
London EC1M 5NR

EU representative: Macmillan Publishers Ireland Limited, 1st Floor, The Liffey Trust Centre,
117-126 Sheriff Street Upper, Dublin 1, D01 YC43
Associated companies throughout the world
www.panmacmillan.com
ISBN: 978-1-5290-6630-2
Text copyright © Justin Roberts 2014
Illustrations copyright © Christian Robinson 2014

Moral rights asserted.

1 3 5 7 9 8 6 4 2

A CIP catalogue record for this book is available from the British Library.

Printed in China

The art for this book was done in coloured pencil.

www.twohootsbooks.com

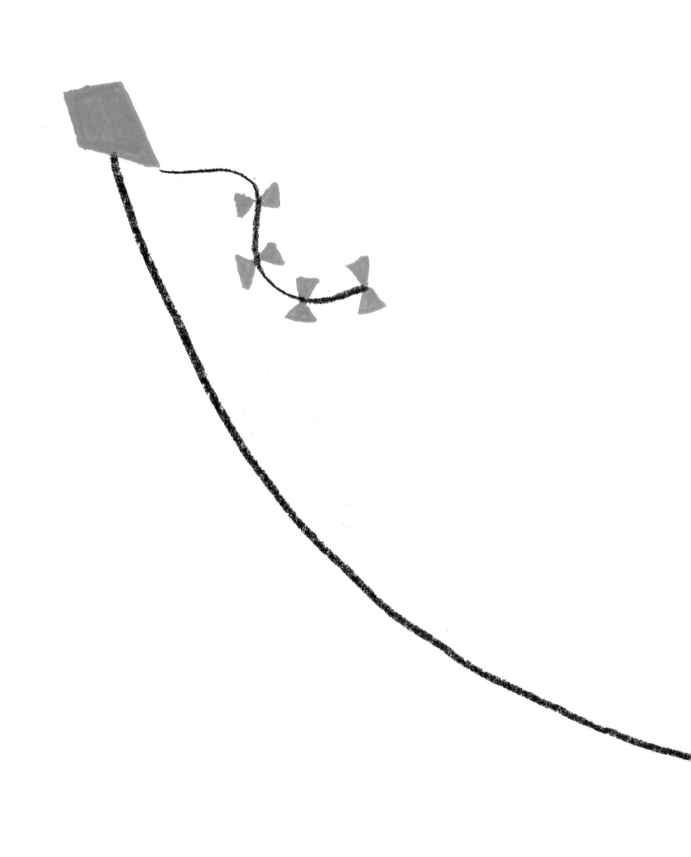

About the author

Justin Roberts is a Grammy-nominated all-star of the family music scene. Hailed by the *New York Times* as "the Judy Blume of kiddie rock," he logs thousands of miles on the road each year, dishing out unexpectedly intelligent and fun rocking music for kids and their parents. Justin lives in Chicago.

About the illustrator

Christian Robinson received a Caldecott Honour and a Coretta Scott King Illustrator Honour for his art in *Last Stop on Market Street*. He is the author and illustrator of the picture books *Another* and *You Matter*, and he has illustrated many more, including *Milo Imagines the World*.